GRIMM
AND
GROSS

Raintree is an imprint of Capstone Global Library Limited, a company incorporated in
England and Wales having its registered office at 264 Banbury Road, Oxford, OX2 7DY –
Registered company number: 6695582

www.raintree.co.uk
myorders@raintree.co.uk

Edited by Eliza Leahy
Designed by Bob Lentz
Original illustrations © Capstone Global Library Limited 2019
Production by Tori Abraham
Originated by Capstone Global Library Ltd
Printed and bound in India

ISBN 978 1 4747 6749 1
22 21 20 19 18
10 9 8 7 6 5 4 3 2 1

British Library Cataloguing in Publication Data
A full catalogue record for this book is available from the British Library.

HANS
IN LUCK

A GRIMM AND GROSS RETELLING

BY J. E. BRIGHT

ILLUSTRATED BY TIMOTHY BANKS

raintree

a Capstone company — publishers for children

CONTENTS

WARNING!

This story stinks. And we mean that in the best possible way. Poor Hans – what a mess! His adventures were bad in the original Grimm tale, but here they're even worse. For starters, imagine a drooling horse, a cow that smells like swamp gas and a pig that never stops farting. And those are his friends! You might not want to reread this story for a while.

 = # GRIM

The Grimm brothers were known for writing some *GRIM* tales. Look for the thumbs-down and you'll know the story is about to get grim.

 = # GROSS

Luckily there's also a lot of *GROSS* stuff in this story. Look for the thumbs-up to see when it's about to get gross.

---

 1. These are footnotes. Get it? Dr Grossius Grimbus, researcher of all things grim and gross, shares his highly scientific observations.

CHAPTER ONE
HORSE LUCK

Hans Pumpernickel knew he was lucky. His mother told him so.

As a baby, he had fallen into a mudslide. *OOZE!* He was rescued by a neighbour's dog.

"Lucky," Frau Pumpernickel said.

As a young boy, Hans got the best grades in his one-room school. His teacher owed his mother money.

"Lucky," said Frau Pumpernickel.

As a teenager, Hans won a boxing championship. The stronger fighters ate bad clams. **GROSS!**

"So very lucky," Frau Pumpernickel said.

But as a young adult, his tiny village had no work for him. Luckily, Hans got a job in the closest big city, Hamsterhaven. It was many miles away. Hans signed a contract with Bert Somersault for seven years of service.

The job was building a new sewer system under the city.

Maybe that part wasn't so lucky.

Still, Hans was happy to have a job. He worked hard for Herr Somersault. He dug through miles of muck and mud.

SQUISH! SQUASH!

He battled hordes of angry biting rats.

SKITTER! SCATTER! SQUEAK!

He connected pipes through which foul things flowed in smelly streams.

GLUG! BLUB! GLOOP!

Every evening before supper, Hans washed in the cold stream behind his servant's shack. But nothing could erase the stink of the sewer.

ong years of hard labour passed

lly, Somersault Construction

the sewer pipe. Herr Somersault was

andsomely.

That night, Hans knocked on the door of his master's cottage.

"Yeth?" Herr Somersault asked. He chewed meat with his mouth open. His breath smelled of sausage.

"Master," said Hans, "I was lucky to work for you. But now the job is done. I'm going home to my mother. Please pay me my wages for the past seven years."

Herr Somersault swallowed. He licked his lips and greasy fingers. *SMACK! SLURP! GLURP!*

He smiled. "You have served me well," he said. Hans smelled mustard on his breath too. "Wait out here."

Hans didn't want to go inside, anyway. His boss's furniture stank like the sewer.

Herr Somersault returned. He handed Hans a solid gold brick! Hans was shocked by how heavy it was.

"Thank you, sir," said Hans. "May your sewer business continue its success."

"Thank you for your good work, Hans," replied Herr Somersault in a gasp of halitosis.[1] **STINK!** "May your life stay lucky. Farewell."

1. Halitosis: the scientific term for bad breath, often caused by chewing garlic, maintaining poor dental hygiene, sucking on dead insects, smoking, coffee, hosting intestinal parasites or eating your mother's awful cooking.

Hans wrapped the gold brick in a handkerchief. He stuck it in his pack, along with some bread. The bag hung heavy on his back. But gold was supposed to be heavy. Hans was lucky to have had such a generous boss.

Hans' mother still lived in the countryside. It was a week's walk away. In the morning, Hans put on his leather cap and set out with his heavy pack. He walked past country houses and farms and fields dotted with cows, sheep and horses. The smell of manure stank up the air. **PEE-YEW!**

It was a beautiful, sunny day. Hans was so lucky! But his backpack felt heavier with every step. His neck became more and more sore.

He trudged up a dirt road to the top of a hill and passed the entrance to a ranch. A sign read THE DOUBLE-A STABLES. Hans heard pounding hooves in the distance. He walked down the road towards an approaching cloud of dust. Out of the cloud raced a chestnut stallion. A middle-aged man rode on its back.

The horse galloped wildly. The rider pulled on the reins. The stallion danced to a stop beside Hans. The horse drooled around the metal bit in his mouth.

The rider wiped the horse drool away with his sleeve. His shirt already had yellow streaks on it. "Hello, traveller!" the man called.

"My name is Aaron Aardvark. Are you coming from Hamsterhaven?"

"Yes, yes," panted Hans, his mouth dry with dust. He put down his pack. His neck and shoulders ached. "I am Hans Pumpernickel. What a fine thing it is to ride, Herr Aardvark! There you sit comfortably. You have no pains from walking."

"Why do you go on foot, then?" Herr Aardvark asked. He stuck his finger in his ear.

"I must," said Hans. "How else can I take my heavy gold brick home to my mother?"

"Why don't we swap?" asked Herr Aardvark. He dug in his ear and pulled out a lump of yellow earwax. "My horse for your brick."

"This is my lucky day!" Hans cheered. "Will you be able to carry the brick home?"

"It's not far," Herr Aardvark replied. He wiped the earwax on his sleeve. *SMEAR!* Then he hopped off the horse.

Hans gave him the gold brick. It was the same colour as the earwax.

Herr Aardvark handed Hans the reins of the bridle.

"The horse's name is Jumper," he explained. "If you want him to go fast, click your tongue and say, 'Jumper, jup, jup!'"

Hans mounted Jumper.

Herr Aardvark lugged the gold brick up the hill.

Hans flicked the reins. Jumper, drooling, strolled down the dusty road.

"I'm the luckiest young man ever," Hans said. He wiped thick horse spittle off his cheek. "Now I'll get home twice as fast!"

CHAPTER TWO
COW LUCK

Hans made good time on Jumper. He reached a ramshackle farmhouse just as the sky turned dark blue. Luckily, the farmer and his wife fed him. They let him stay the night in the hayloft over the barn. His horse was safe and warm, drooling in the stable below.

Late in the night, Hans woke to an eerie sound. *"WHOO! WHOO! WHOO!"* At first he thought it was the wind. He pulled more itchy straw on top of himself to keep warm.

But then Hans felt a drip on his face.

He sat up and stared into the darkness of the hayloft rafters. "Who's there?" he croaked.

"**WHOO! WHOO!**" hooted a barn owl. He flapped his heavy wings. And then he squirted more droppings onto Hans' head.

Hans wiped the stinky owl goo from his face. "I sure am lucky!" he exclaimed. "At least it's not a cow up there." Then he covered his face with his leather cap. He burrowed as deeply as he could into the straw and slept uncomfortably until dawn.

23

Hans woke groggy. He thanked the farmer and his wife. Jumper carried him down the road again.

It was a slow, long, dreary day. The landscape was boring fields. The road was flat. The sky was grey. Even the chirping of the sparrows in the scrubby trees became irritating.

"CHEEP, CHEEP, CHEEP!"

Hans rode listlessly on Jumper for hours. The biggest excitement came when Jumper drooled too much. Hans wiped the horse dribble with a rag on a stick.

Hans was lulled by the dull ride. He barely noticed when the grey sky grew darker. But then he realized there was only an hour left of daylight! They were far from any shelter. Jumper needed to go faster!

 This is where it gets GROSS!

Hans clicked his tongue. "Jumper," he ordered. "Jup! Jup!"

Jumper took off at full gallop. He clopped at a breakneck clip down the road.

In the saddle, Hans bounced around wildly. Spews of drool from Jumper's mouth caught the wind and smacked against Hans' face.

SPLASH!

A string of dribble wet his arm.

SPLOSH!

Then a great glob of the horse saliva slimed Hans' eyes.

SPLAT!

Hans struggled to stay upright on the racing beast. He let go of the reins to clear his eyes. So he saw Jumper thundering past a woman leading a cow along the roadside.

The cow mooed. Jumper reared up and whirled around.

Hans was thrown off the horse.

The world spun crazily as Hans flipped

through the air. His leather cap flew into the road. **WHAM!**

Hans landed on his back in a muddy ditch filled with wriggling tadpoles.

Hans stared up at the dark grey sky. He was soaked by drool and cold slime. His rear end would be sore for days.

He must be lucky to survive such a terrible fall!

Hans climbed to his feet. He wobbled on his bruised legs. Down the road, Jumper had stopped beside the old woman and her cow.

The woman led the cow and Jumper to him. She picked up his cap on the way.

"Nasty fall," said the woman. She was skinny and frail. Hans saw her long, dirty fingernails as she handed him his cap. "Perhaps you shouldn't ride so fast."

Hans narrowed his eyes. "It is a poor joke, this riding," he said. "Jumper runs so wild and drools so much. I was lucky that I didn't break my neck! Never again will I ride him."

"You can see by his mouth foam he has a feisty spirit," said the woman. She scraped her long nails along Jumper's side. The horse quivered and dribbled.

"Not like your quiet cow," said Hans. He put on his cap. "You walked calmly beside her. She gives milk for butter and cheese. Anyone would be lucky to have such a cow."

The old woman scratched a hair on her chin with her talons. "Well," she said, "maybe it's your lucky day after all. I do not mind trading the cow for the horse."

"Wonderful!" exclaimed Hans. He took the cow's lead rope from the woman's claw.

The woman vaulted onto Jumper's back with shocking skill. "Jup! Jup!" she shouted. The horse galloped away. The woman waved her long-nailed hand at Hans as she left him in the dust.

With a sigh of relief, Hans started walking along the road with his cow. He decided to name her Bertha.

Bertha chewed her cud as she ambled beside him. She let out a deep burp and mooed in satisfaction.

Hans grinned as the sun began to set. "I will travel more slowly. But now I can have butter and cheese when I want! If I get thirsty, I have milk to drink. I could even sell the dairy products and make a nice living for mother and myself. What more could I want?" Hans asked himself happily. "I must be the luckiest young man in the world."

Bertha mooed and belched again.

CHAPTER THREE
PIG LUCK

Hans and Bertha didn't reach an inn before nightfall. Instead Hans found an empty shack on the side of the road. Wind whistled through the missing slats in the walls. Bugs buzzed under the rotten wooden floorboards. Bertha snored all night. But Hans felt lucky as he slept beside the cow on the hard floor. She kept him warm. Although she kept burping into his face and fluttering his eyelashes with her smelly gusts.

In the morning, Bertha ate grass. Hans ate

the last of his stale bread. He was worried that he had run out. The next inn they found would surely have food.

Hans and Bertha set off down the dusty road. At their slow pace, they still had many days of walking to go.

The day grew hotter as the sun rose overhead. By noon, the road shimmered with waves of heat. The surrounding land was flat, dry and rocky. He was grateful for his cap keeping the sun off his head.

Bertha burped constantly. Her belches smelled of swamp gas.

BUUUURP!

This is where it gets pretty GRIM*!*

Hans' mouth dried out in the heat. The more he sweated, the thirstier he felt. His tongue felt like sandpaper. His lips cracked. But there was no water anywhere. The landscape around them looked like the surface of the moon.

After a few miles, Hans realized that he had the solution. Bertha! "I'll milk her now," he gasped. "I'll refresh myself with her cool milk."

Hans tied Bertha's rope to a dead, twisted tree trunk. He had no pail, so Hans held his leather cap under Bertha's udder.

Clumsily, Hans tried to milk Bertha. He squeezed and pulled. No liquid came out. So he squeezed harder.

Bertha burped. She shifted and mooed in distress.

Hans was so thirsty. He pulled on the cow's udder as hard as he could.

The cow raised her back hoof. With a loud belch, she kicked Hans in his head.

CLANG!

The kick sounded like a ringing bell in Hans' ears. He saw twinkling cows dancing around him. Hans fell over, knocked out.

It was a good thing Hans was so lucky. When he opened his eyes, a podgy young man around his own age pushed a wheelbarrow up the dusty road. There were streaks of blood on the man's white jacket. A squirming pig rode inside the wheelbarrow.

Hans tried to sit up. He saw dancing cows again and fell over.

"Hello! Are you hurt?" the bloody man yelled at Hans. He parked his wheelbarrow and helped Hans sit up.

"My cow, Bertha," Hans gasped. His mouth was more parched than ever. "She kicked me! I tried to milk her so I could have a drink."

The man pulled a canteen from his pack. He handed it to Hans. "Here, drink some of my cool water from a stream."

Hans drank. He spat out a wriggling minnow. But he was thirsty enough to take another gulp.

The man circled Bertha, inspecting her. "Hello!" he said again. It wasn't a greeting so much as a shout of surprise. "My name is Herman Frankfurter. I work as a butcher. This cow is very old indeed. She couldn't give milk if she wanted to."

Bertha burped.

"No wonder she kicked," said Hans. "I'm lucky she didn't knock the life out of me."

"Yep," said Herr Frankfurter. "She is fit only for pulling a plough . . . or being turned into steak."

Bertha belched in alarm. The pig in the wheelbarrow squealed and passed gas.

PFFFFFT!

"I do not care much for beef," said Hans. He took another sip of water. He spat out a second minnow. "Beef is not juicy enough for me. I prefer . . . pork sausage." Hans glanced over at the pig. Again the pig broke wind.

"Hello!" said Herr Frankfurter. "I have a terrific idea. We shall trade the pig for the cow. Then we will both be pleased."

"That would be so good of you," said Hans. "Let us make the exchange."

Hans took the wheelbarrow with the young, gassy pig.

Herman took the rope tied to Bertha, the old, burping cow.

"Thank you!" cried Hans. He steered the pig down the road. "May the future repay your kindness! May your luck be as good as mine!"

CHAPTER FOUR
GOOSE LUCK

After much travelling, Hans finally reached a greener, cooler valley. There he rested on the grassy bank of a stream with his pig. He had named her Dumpling. Dumpling farted and took a nap.

Not long after, a young woman arrived. She had yellow hair and a red nose. Under one arm she carried a plump white goose.

"Greetings," said Hans.

"ACHOO!" sneezed the woman. She wiped her nose, which was runny. "Hi dere," she said. Her words sounded muffled by her cold. "By name is Bary Gesundheit. I deed somb water."

Hans stood up and moved back a little. He didn't want to be close to the sick woman. "Go ahead," he told her. "The stream is refreshing and safe to drink."

Bary Gesundheit – although Hans guessed her first name was really Mary – put the goose down on the grass. While the bird flapped her wings, Frau Gesundheit cupped water into her hand and drank it. She sat up. Frau Gesundheit had a big green snot bubble coming out of one nostril.

"I am a lucky man," Hans said. "I have made such good bargains on my journey."

"Oh yeth?" Frau Gesundheit said, sniffing. "How pleasant for you. I'm daking this goose to by brother's wedding. Be bill eat it at the feast."

"She does look plump and delicious," said Hans.

"Liff her uh," said Frau Gesundheit. "Liff her!"

So Hans took hold of the goose's wings. He hoisted the bird in the air. "Huh," said Hans. "Very heavy."

"I'b beeh faddening her for the bast six weeks," Frau Gesundheit explained. "She'll be juicy and belicious and eberyone will day I brought the best weddink bift."

"She is a generous present for your brother," agreed Hans. He put the goose down. He was already thinking how lucky he would be to bring a goose home to his mother instead of a pig. A goose was much easier to carry than pushing flatulent Dumpling in the wheelbarrow. "My pig is heavier, though."

 It gets GROSS *AND* GRIM *here!*

Dumpling farted.

Frau Gesundheit took out a handkerchief and blew her nose. She sprayed snot in the air. Hans ducked to avoid getting splashed with mucus.

"I have bad news for you," said Frau Gesundheit. Her voice was clearer now. "Your pig might be suspicious."

"What could you mean?" asked Hans.

MISSING

"Known for rude toots"
★ ★ ★

"In the last village I passed," Frau Gesundheit explained, "the people searched for a stolen pig. It was taken from the mayor's sty. I fear that this is that missing pig. It was famous for its rude toots."[2]

"I didn't steal Dumpling!" cried Hans. "I traded Bertha for her fair and square!"

"I'm telling you how it looks," said Frau Gesundheit. "The townspeople may arrest you."

"Oh no!" cried Hans.

2. Farmers all over the county set out to find this gaseous hog most notably *because* of its rude toots. The pig's toots were so great that they could be captured and turned into energy. They could power a whole farm!

"We will have to trade," said Frau Gesundheit. "The pig will make a fine wedding gift doo, and I'm heading in the bother birection." She sniffed loudly. "The other direction. With the goose, you won't get into trouble."

"Oh, thank you!" said Hans. He quickly traded the goose for Dumpling and the wheelbarrow. Frau Gesundheit blew her nose again. Then she pushed the cart away down the road.

Hans smiled. "I am so lucky. What a great deal I have made. A goose is as delicious as a pig. Also it has soft white feathers to stuff a pillow!"

As Hans started to walk again on his journey home, the goose honked. "Wait," she said. "You should know that I have magic powers!"

"Oh yes?" asked Hans.

"Yes!" squawked the bird. "I am the goose that lays golden eggs."

"You keep that to yourself," said Hans. "I don't care. I've had enough of gold. It's too heavy. I'm lucky it's gone."

CHAPTER FIVE
STONE LUCK

The goose's name was Oro. Hans carried her under his arm. They made good time over the next few days. Although Oro got even heavier as she held on to her golden eggs.

Finally, they reached a village called Grubb. It was the last little town before his mother's country farm.

In Grubb's village square, Hans stopped at the fountain for a drink. Beside the fountain was a skinny scissors grinder and his cart.

The young man was noisily sharpening a knife on his whirling whetstone.

Hans watched the scissors grinder work. Beautiful sparks flew from the stone as the man sharpened the knife. The grinder grinned. His bare arms shined with a red, scaly rash.

The man finished sharpening the blade. Hans said, "You are lucky to be so merry with your occupation! My name is Hans. This is my goose, Oro."

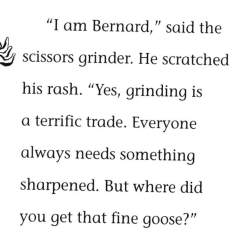

"I am Bernard," said the scissors grinder. He scratched his rash. "Yes, grinding is a terrific trade. Everyone always needs something sharpened. But where did you get that fine goose?"

"Oh, I traded a pig for her," Hans explained.

"Where did you get the pig?" asked Bernard.

"I exchanged a cow for the pig," said Hans.

"Where did you get the cow?" asked Bernard.

"I traded my horse for it," said Hans.

"And the horse?" asked Bernard. He itched his patchy rash.

"For the horse I traded a brick of gold," said Hans.

"Wherever did you get so much gold?" asked Bernard.

"Well," said Hans, "that was my pay for seven years' labour digging a sewer."

"You have made excellent trades," said

Bernard. "Now you need a way to make money whenever you need it."

"How could I be that lucky?" asked Hans.

"You could trade your goose for this grindstone," said Bernard. "Then you can sharpen knives and scissors and anything else people need sharpened. You'll always have well-paying work."

"That is the best deal yet!" exclaimed Hans. He gave Bernard the goose. Bernard gave him the big, heavy whetstone wheel.

Hans lugged the whetstone out of Grubb. He staggered down the road towards his mother's farm. "There is nobody luckier than me," Hans told himself. "I must have been born under a shooting star."

Hans hauled the whetstone for another few miles. His arms ached from its weight. He got thirsty again. The sun was hot. There was no shade.

Herr Howler's beet farm was just down the road from Hans' mother's small turnip field. There Hans stopped at a stone well. He panted from exhaustion and thirst. Gasping, he put the whetstone down on the well's short wall.

Hans turned the crank to raise the well's water bucket. He took a big gulp. Then he let go of the bucket.

The bucket hit the edge of the whetstone.

BONK!

The whetstone rocked. It fell into the well. Hans heard it plop into the water below.

SPLASH!

The water in the well was full of slimy algae. Hans got covered in it. He felt sick that he had drunk the goop.

Then he realized the whetstone was gone.

Forever. He stared down into the well, shocked by its loss.

Then Hans jumped to his feet. He danced with joy. Tears sprang to his eyes. "Thank you, wonderful luck!" he cried. "My heavy burden was taken from me. And it wasn't my fault!"

Hans spun around. He laughed at how light he felt. He had nothing, and had never felt more carefree. "I am the luckiest man under the sun," he sang. "I am the most fortunate one!"

With a happy heart, Hans ran home. There he was reunited with his mother at last.

THE END

COMPARING THE TALES

After reading J. E. Bright's retelling of this weird Grimm Brothers tale, you won't think Hans is lucky at all! He spends his teenage years fighting rats and gunk while building a sewage system. And back in the Grimms' day, workers didn't have backhoes and cranes and automatic drills. Hans does everything by hand. In the sewer. For seven years. You call that lucky?

In the original tale, Hans is given a lump of silver for all his hard work. (Maybe health benefits would have been a better deal.) But Bright turns the treasure gold. Gold is much heavier than silver, so it makes sense it would be hard for Hans to carry.

All the animals in the Grimms' tale are described as being "fine". Hmmmm.

Bright gives the creatures in his story some real personalities. As well as character flaws. Like farting and drooling. But Hans sees the best in everyone around him, and that includes the animals.

Bright sticks to the original ending. Poor Hans! His mother is waiting for him at the end. Let's hope she doesn't find out what her "lucky" son lost. She could have bought a lot of cool stuff with that gold. And a gassy pig would've at least given them bacon for breakfast.

GLOSSARY

distress in urgent need of help

gallop run so fast that all four legs leave the ground at once

generous willing to share

handsomely more than a good amount

hayloft platform high above the floor of a barn where hay is stored

labour work

landscape large area of land

podgy short and plump

stallion adult male horse

whetstone stone used to sharpen blades

GROSSARY

BELCH let out gases in your stomach through your mouth with a loud noise

EARWAX yellow or orange substance made inside the ears

FLATULENT gassy or farting a lot

FOUL something very unpleasant to the eyes, nose or mouth

GREASY oily

MANURE animal waste

MUCUS sticky or slimy fluid that coats and protects the inside of the nose, throat, lungs and other parts of the body

OOZE leak out slowly

RASH area of skin that becomes red, itchy or irritated

SALIVA clear liquid in your mouth that helps you swallow and begin to digest food

SEWER system, often underground pipes, that carries away liquid and solid waste

TOOT fart

DISCUSS

1. Hans calls himself the luckiest man under the sun. Talk about a time you've felt lucky. Have you ever had good luck like Hans?

2. A lot of Hans' trades were pretty gross. Which of the things he traded for do you think was the grossest?

3. Hans goes on a long trip to see his mother in the countryside. How would you feel if you had to walk all the way out into the country?

WRITE

1. Frau Gesundheit talks with a very stuffy nose. Try writing a sentence in her voice. For example, "I've been fattening her up for the past six weeks" is written like "I'b beeh faddening her for the bast six weeks." Say your sentence out loud and see if it sounds like you have a cold!

2. Hans makes a lot of trades during the story. Write about a time you traded for something better.

3. Hans went through a lot on his way to his mother. Write a letter from Hans' perspective explaining to his mother what the worst part of his trip was.

AUTHOR

J. E. BRIGHT is the writer of many novels, novelizations and novelty books for children and young adults. He lives in Texas, USA, with his cuddly female cat, Mabel, and his friendly dog, Henry. Find out more about J. E. Bright on his website.

ILLUSTRATOR

TIMOTHY BANKS is an award-winning artist and illustrator from South Carolina, USA. He's created character designs for Nike, Nickelodeon and Cartoon Network, quirky covers for *Paste* magazine and lots of children's books with titles such as *There's a Norseman in My Classroom* and *The Frankenstein Journals*.

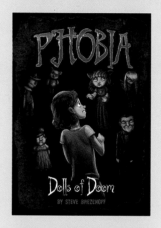

a Capstone company — publishers for children